The Tickety Tale Teller

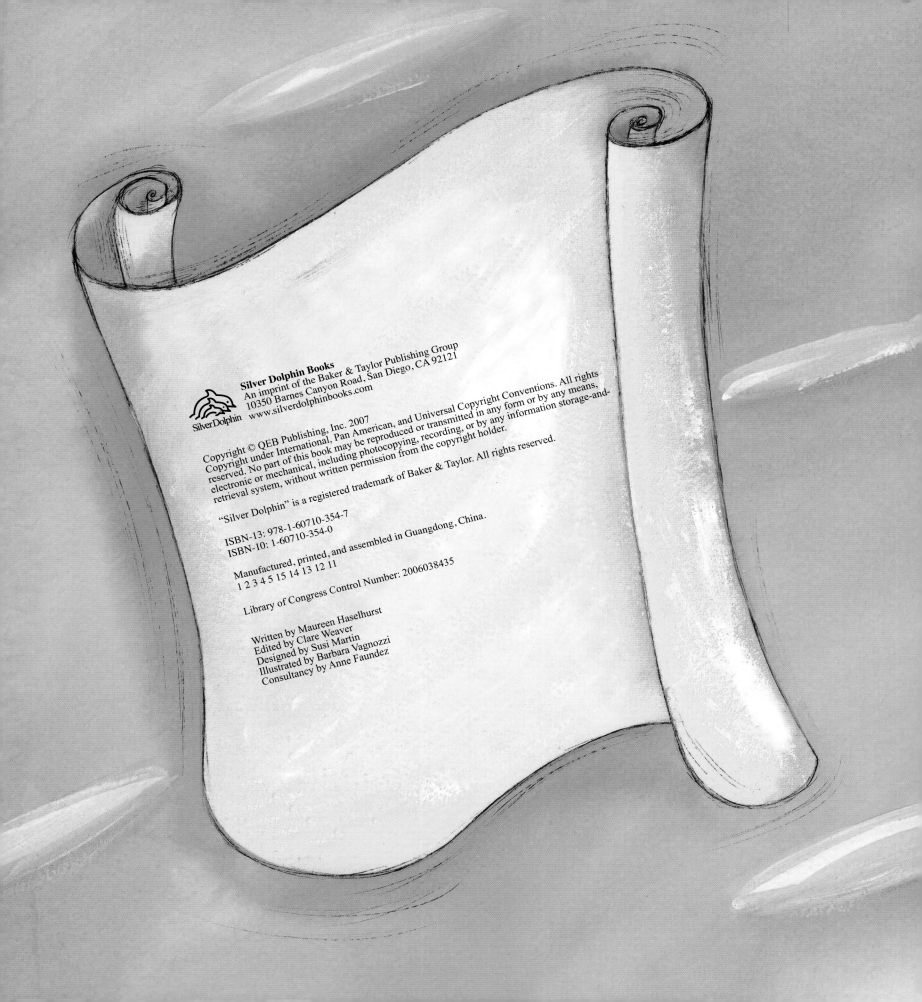

Silver Dolphin Books
An imprint of the Baker & Taylor Publishing Group
10350 Barnes Canyon Road, San Diego, CA 92121
www.silverdolphinbooks.com

ISBN-13: 978-1-60710-354-7
ISBN-10: 1-60710-354-0

Manufactured, printed, and assembled in Guangdong, China.
1 2 3 4 5 15 14 13 12 11

Library of Congress Control Number: 2006038435

Written by Maureen Haselhurst
Edited by Clare Weaver
Designed by Susi Martin
Illustrated by Barbara Vagnozzi
Consultancy by Anne Faundez

The Tickety Tale Teller

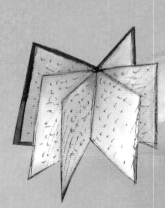

Maureen Haselhurst

Illustrated by
Barbara Vagnozzi

Silver Dolphin

San Diego, California

Once, in a faraway town, there was a sky-high tower called Tall Stories and in it lived the

Tickety Tale Teller.

Over many long years,
she had filled the rooms
with her wonderful tales,
until Tall Stories was
bursting with books.

Whenever the children in the town
below wanted to hear a story, they
would fly a flag from their window.

A dragon flag for a fairy story,
a star flag for a space story,
a ship for a pirate story, and so on.

Every day, the Tickety Tale Teller would look down at the flags from her sky-high tower and say to herself,

"Another story, quickety-quick! I'll be there in a tickety-tick,"

and grabbing a bundle of books, she would slide, helter-skelter down her banister and scoot out the door.

She became busier and busier. Everyone wanted a story. Bedtimes were a hurly-burly of comings and goings as she scurried from house to house.

The poor Tickety Tale Teller
was working so hard, she could
barely keep up!

It would be so much easier if she could
tell all the children a story at the same
time—but how? She had an idea!

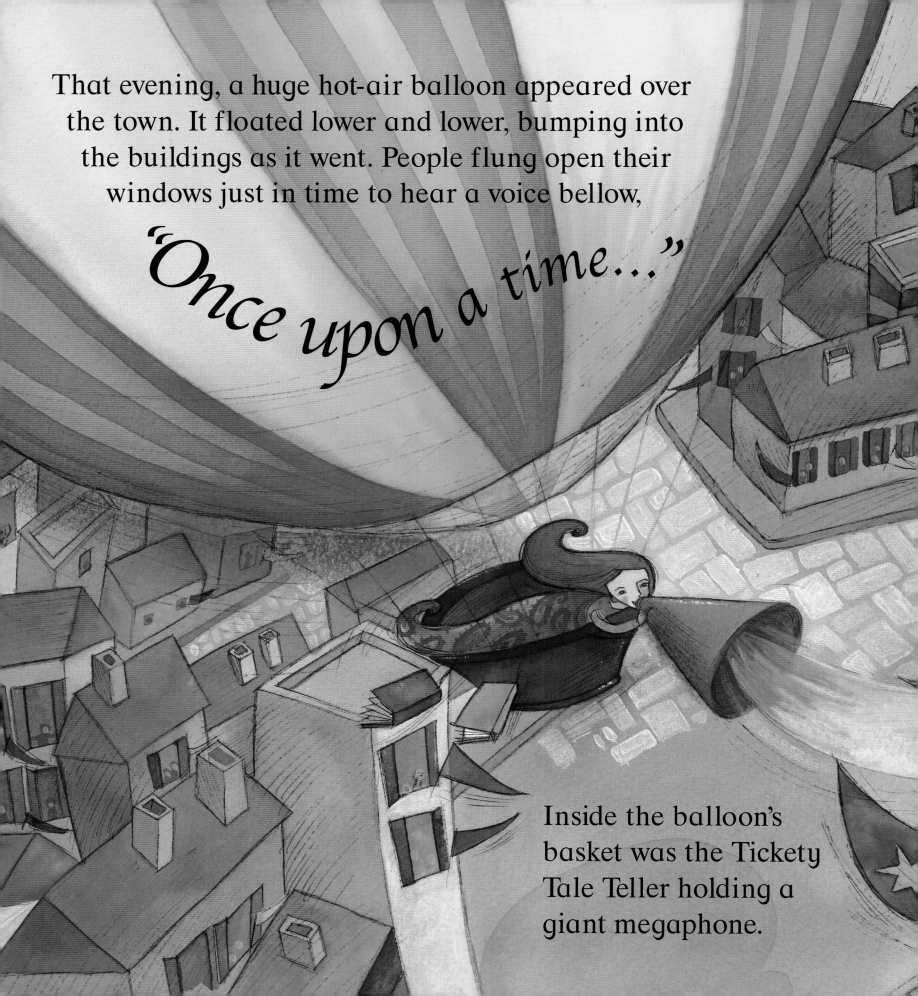

That evening, a huge hot-air balloon appeared over the town. It floated lower and lower, bumping into the buildings as it went. People flung open their windows just in time to hear a voice bellow,

"Once upon a time..."

Inside the balloon's basket was the Tickety Tale Teller holding a giant megaphone.

"Please go away!"
shouted the children.
"You're waking us up!
Besides, we want to be
read a story the right way."

She went away.

No problem, she
already had
another idea.

The following evening,
great glittering fountains of sparks
glowed in the sky above the town.

Fireworks!

People flung open their windows
as a bright finger of fire wrote,

"Once upon a time..."

and then fizzled out as the
air whooshed and whizzed
and whirly-gigged.

"Please go away!"

shouted the children. "You're waking
us up! Besides, we want to be
told a story the right way."

For many days, no one saw the Tickety Tale Teller. The children flew their story flags but she never came.

Do not disturb

Inside Tall Stories there
was a flurry of housework
as, room by room, the
Tickety Tale Teller cleared
the shelves of books.

The following morning, a carnival float rumbled through the town, fluttering with flags and banners, and heaped with brightly wrapped packages.

Out jumped the Tickety Tale Teller and she scooted from door to door, popping a package into every mailbox.

Inside each package
was a storybook with
a note saying,

Please read this tale
to the children
—until they can
read it to you.

And so it was that everyone in the town became a storyteller. It was now their turn to fill Tall Stories with tales of their own.

As for the Tickety Tale Teller, it was
time to move on to another town.

Climbing into her balloon, she floated away,

scattering a trail of brightly
wrapped tales.

Notes for Parents and Teachers

- Using shoe boxes, build a model Tall Stories tower. Fill the rooms with books of different genres. Ask the children to write a story of their own to be stored in a special "room" at the top of the tower. Using blocks, etc., build a town at the foot of the tower and choose a name for it. Encourage the children to imagine what might happen in their town. Who lives there? Who built it? What goes on there?

- Design flags with pictures to tell the Tickety Tale Teller what kind of tales the children would like to hear. Display the flags on a clothesline.

- If the children have access to a slide, they can pretend to be the Tickety Tale Teller sliding down her banister and chanting, "Another story, quickety-quick! I'll be there in a tickety-tick."

- Make a model hot-air balloon using a helium-filled balloon. The basket can be made from a painted egg carton. Suspend it with ribbons, wool, or string. Decorate the balloon with aluminum foil, ribbons, and feathers. Hang it from the ceiling or a window frame.

- Create a collage of a firework display using colored foil, glitter, and sequins against a dark background. Ask the children to think of words to describe what they would see, hear, smell, and how they would feel. Include the words on the collage. In music class, compose firework music with drums, tambourines, triangles, whistles, kazoos, and other instruments.

- Sort through the bookshelves and ask each child to choose a favorite book, the title of which they must keep secret. Then they gift wrap their choice. Each piece of gift wrap is labeled in advance with the name of another child. When the packages are opened, the children read their book (or have it read to them) and then guess who might have chosen that book.

- Play the Tickety Tale memory game. Collect items from the story—for example, book, sparkler, gift wrap, flag, balloon. Have the children study the items for one minute and then cover the items with a cloth. How many items can the children remember?

- Make a Tickety Snakes and Ladders game. Use banisters as snakes and stairs as ladders. Tiny wrapped packages could be used as counters.

- Set up a story chain—one child begins to tell a story, which is then taken over by the next child, and so on, until it reaches its conclusion. Some children will be more comfortable retelling a familiar story, while others will be confident enough to create their own.

- Have a pass-the-package story session, using a bag containing several books. When the music stops, the children chant, "With a tickety-tick, choose a story, quickety-quick! Close your eyes and take your pick." The child holding the bag chooses a story, which is read aloud either by the adult or by the child, and the process is repeated.